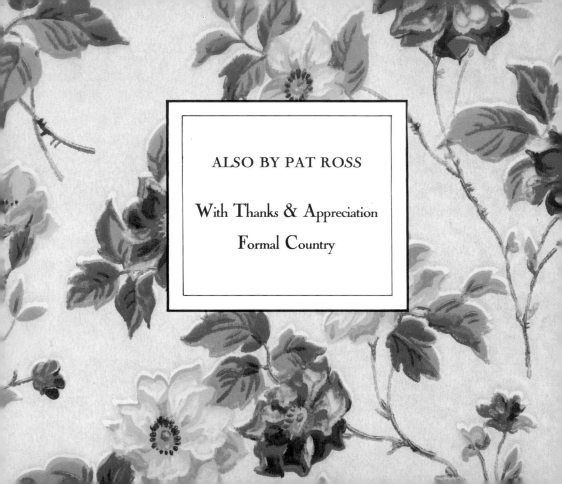

ALSO BY PAT ROSS

With Thanks & Appreciation

Formal Country

The Pleasure of
Your Company

To _____

From _____

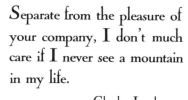

Separate from the pleasure of your company, I don't much care if I never see a mountain in my life.

—Charles Lamb,
in a letter to
William Wordsworth,
1801

The Pleasure of Your Company

The Sweet Nellie Book of Traditional Sentiments and Customs of Proper Entertaining

PAT ROSS

VIKING
STUDIO
BOOKS

VIKING STUDIO BOOKS
Published by the Penguin Group
Viking Penguin, a division of Penguin Books USA Inc.,
40 West 23rd Street, New York, New York 10010, U.S.A.
Penguin Books Ltd, 27 Wrights Lane, London W8 5TZ, England
Penguin Books Australia Ltd, Ringwood, Victoria, Australia
Penguin Books Canada Ltd, 2801 John Street, Markham, Ontario, Canada L3R 1B4
Penguin Books (N.Z.) Ltd, 182–190 Wairau Road, Auckland 10, New Zealand

Penguin Books Ltd, Registered Offices: Harmondsworth, Middlesex, England

First published in 1989 by Viking Penguin, a division of Penguin Books USA Inc.

1 3 5 7 9 10 8 6 4 2

Grateful acknowledgment is made for permission to reprint "The Perfect
Hostess," "The Perfect Guest," and "Vers de Societe" from The Perfect
Hostess by Rose Henniker Heaton. By permission of Methuen & Co.

LIBRARY OF CONGRESS CATALOGING IN PUBLICATION DATA
Ross, Pat.
The pleasure of your company : the Sweet Nellie book of
traditional sentiments and customs of proper entertaining /
Pat Ross   ;   text with Leisa Crane.
p.   cm.
ISBN 0-670-83038-0
1. Entertaining—Quotations, maxims, etc.   I. Crane, Leisa.
II. Title.
BJ2021.R67   1989
395'.3—dc20   89-40359

Printed in Japan   Set in Nicholas Cochin
Designed by Amy Hill.

AN APPRECIATION

With each new book, there are always many colleagues, friends, and family members to thank once again. My sincere appreciation both to those who contributed their time and expertise and those who made up the support section. Particular gratitude goes to the following: Leisa Crane, for her fine research and good cheer; the enthusiastic staff at Sweet Nellie; Berta Montgomery, for the lovely vintage wallpaper; the many ephemera dealers—Marjorie Adams, Bernice Stewart, and Bonnie Ferris, especially—who hunted through their files for us; Arlene Kirkwood, for loaning us her wonderful dance card collection; Carolyn Gore, for loaning us her wonderful old family scrapbooks; the many librarians and antiquarian booksellers who were never too busy to answer endless questions; Amy Berkower, my agent; my family, for sacrificing the dining-room table; and, of course, everyone at Viking Studio Books, most particularly Michael Fragnito, Barbara Williams, Emily Kuenstler, and Amy Hill for coming through with yet another special book.

INTRODUCTION

The role of being host or guest as part of an enjoyable, lifelong tradition of entertaining begins in childhood. Who cannot remember inviting friends for a birthday party or an overnight of giggling long past lights-out? I can recall tea parties under tall, broad-leafed trees, with tiny chipped cups and saucers ("Chip and Dale," we called the set, without really knowing why it was funny) and friends dressed up in their parents' finery. I loved playing the hostess because the role allowed a certain degree of proper ceremony and required an impressive knowledge of the rules of teatime. We have grown up, but the joy of having a guest and being a guest continues.

It is exhilarating to be a part of a generation of people who enjoy entertaining. The bookstore shelves are overflowing with volumes on a wealth of such topics, from giving picnics and barbecues to celebrating, with style, the major events of our lives. When we cook, have weekend guests, or dine and dance with friends, we carry on traditions that are age old and cherished. It is still important to most of us that we honor old-fashioned good manners so that our entertainment will be memorable to both friends and acquaintances.

My teenage daughter listens with some amusement as I tell her about the dance cards that I wore tied around my wrist when I was her age. I knew the time and the place for long white gloves, endless receiving lines at parties, and dancing at a polite distance when the adults were looking. I have fond memories of the many rules of politeness that made our lives seem orderly and happily predictable. Though our definition of hospitality and entertaining is far more casual today than it was in the past, people still appreciate being treated well.

The Pleasure of Your Company celebrates the many ways past generations paid attention to the details of etiquette as they went about having a good time. Traditional manners may have faded and been modified, but they have not been lost to us, as modern as we may seem.

The Well-Bred Hostess

THE PERFECT
HOSTESS

She makes you feel when you arrive
How good it is to be alive.
She promptly orders fresh-made tea
However late the hour may be.
She leads you to a comfy room
With fire ablaze—and flowers abloom.
She shows you cupboards large and wide,
No hats or frocks of *hers* inside!
A writing-table meets your eye,
The newest novels on it lie.
The bed is just a nest of down,
Her maid puts out your dinner-gown.
The water's hot from morn till night,
Her dinners fill you with delight.

She never makes you stand for hours
Admiring children, dogs or flowers!
What better way to please her guest?
The Perfect Hostess lets you rest.

—Elizabeth Paget, in
The Perfect Hostess
Rose Henniker Heaton
1931

The ideal hostess must have so many perfections of sense and character that were she described in full, no one seemingly but a combination of seer and angel could ever hope to qualify.

—*Etiquette*
Emily Post
1922

Hospitality consists of a little fire, a little food, and an immense quiet.

—*Journals*
Ralph Waldo Emerson
1856

House beautiful—your book, from end to end,
And every page a room to lodge a friend;
Fain would I enter with a seemly grace,
Attired and mannered as befits the place;
But best endeavor falls below the aim
And rests at last, content to leave a name.

—*The Album Writer's Friend*
J.S. Ogilvie
1881

Stay is a charming word in a friend's vocabulary.

—*Concord Days*
Amos Bronson Alcott
1872

A good hostess is like a life guard at a summer resort, who usually seems to be doing nothing but loll on the beach—until someone starts to drown.

—*The Entertaining Lady*
Vera Bloom
1949

Let a hostess remember one thing: there is no chance for vivacity of intellect if her room is too warm; her flowers and her guests will wilt together.

—*Manners & Social Usage*
Mrs. John Sherwood
1884

A most charming woman, Madame Récamier could make every guest feel as if he were the particular shining star of her salon merely by murmuring *"En fin!"* ("At last!") when he came, and *"Déjà?"* ("So soon?") when he left.

—*The Entertaining Lady*
Vera Bloom
1949

LITTLE COMFORTS FOR
THE GUEST ROOM

 iscuits.

Matches and cigarette ash-tray.

Pincushion with plenty of different kinds of pins.

Needles threaded with black and white cotton.

 Aspirins.

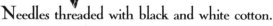

Gas or electric fire, with kettle and small saucepan.

Plenty of coat-hangers.

Mushrooms for hats.

Some spare trees for shoes.

All writing material, and a board in case
she likes writing in bed.

Reading lamp.

A wide choice of books.

Her favourite magazines.

—*The Perfect Hostess*
Rose Henniker Heaton
1931

The Gracious Guest

THE PERFECT
GUEST

She answered by return of post
    The invitation of her host
She caught the train she said she would
And changed at junctions as she should.
She brought a light and smallish box
And keys belonging to the locks.
Food, strange and rare, she did not beg,
But ate the homely scrambled egg.
When offered lukewarm tea she drank it.
She did not crave an extra blanket,
Nor extra pillows for her head:
She seemed to like the spare-room bed.
She never came downstairs till ten,
She brought her own self-filling pen,

Nor once by look or word of blame
Exposed her host to open shame.
She left no little things behind,
Excepting . . . loving thoughts and kind.

—*The Perfect Hostess*
Rose Henniker Heaton
1931

A common error into which women (and especially young girls) fall when going away for a short visit is in regard to the enormous amount of luggage they take with them. This occasion proves a source of actual annoyance to the hostess, especially if the luggage is of a large and bulky nature.

—*The Woman's Book:*
Contains Everything a
Woman Ought to Know
Florence B. Jack
1911

If you have a tiresome guest who insists upon following you around and weighing heavily on your hands, be firm, go to your own room, and lock the door. If you have a sulky guest who looks bored, throw open the library-door, order the carriage, and make your own escape. But if you have a very agreeable guest who shows every desire to please and be pleased, give that model guest the privilege of choosing her own hours and her own retirement.

—*Manners & Social Usage*
Mrs. John Sherwood
1884

Fish and visitors stink in three days.

—*Poor Richard's Almanack*
Benjamin Franklin
1736

Unbidden guests
Are often welcomest when they are gone.

—*The First Part of
King Henry the Sixth*
William Shakespeare
1591

If you are a visitor be careful to keep your room as neat as possible. Do not let garments lie scattered about promiscuously.

—*American Etiquette
and Rules of Politeness*
A. E. Davis
1882

Never pick your teeth, clean your nails, scratch your head or pick your nose in company.

—*American Etiquette
and Rules of Politeness*
A. E. Davis
1882

If one can do so without ostentation, it is a pretty courtesy to a hostess to send her some little souvenir of your visit, a new book, a deck of cards in a handsome case, a bit of handwork if you embroider, some new music you know will be acceptable, etc.

—*"Dame Curtsey's" Book of Novel
Entertainments for Every Day in the Year*
Ellye Howell Glover
1907

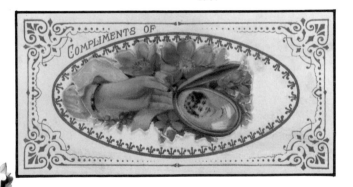

It was a delightful visit—perfect in being much too short.

—*Emma*
Jane Austen
1816

VERS DE SOCIÉTÉ
Any Guest to Any Hostess

Dear Hostess, Let me write a line to say
    How greatly we enjoyed our [little] stay.
                  [lengthy]
Our [cheery] visit, lots of [luscious] food
    [quiet]   [simple]
Have done us both a *frightful* lot of good.
The [shooting and fishing] you provided
    [ping pong and the tennis]
My [husband]
    [brother] revelled in them, just as <u>I</u> did!
    [nephew]
Our fellow-guests were such a pleasant feature
We thought [the Duchess a most charming] creature.
    [the Vicar a most earnest]

I hope that we may shortly have the pleasure
Of seeing you [up north] when you have leisure.
      [down south]
P.S.—*So sorry!* Hope you do not mind,
I find I left my [shooting stick] behind.
      [fishing rod]
      [waterproof]
      [knitting bag]
      [hot-water bottle]

—*The Perfect Hostess*
Rose Henniker Heaton
1931

The Taking of Tea

ea, thou soft, thou sober, sage and venerable drink. . . .

—*The Lady's Last Stake*
Colley Cibber
1708

I must further advise you, Harriet, not to heap such mountains of sugar in your tea, nor to pour such a deluge of cream into it. People will certainly take you for the daughter of a dairymaid!

—*To Think of Tea*
Agnes Repplier
1932

It may be noted here that everybody does not know how to make good tea. The tea itself should be of the very best quality. Nothing is worse than cheap tea.

To be able to talk to guests and pour out tea and coffee—perhaps to flavor them as well—all at the same time demands great nimbleness of wits.

No gentleman who is giving a tea, reception or entertainment of any kind should endeavor to detain a young girl after the chaperon has left.

—Good Manners for All Occasions
Margaret E. Sangstep
1904

In happy homes where tea is brewed at five o'clock, or where, indeed, it is always on tap, life is a success.

—*Manners & Social Usage*
Mrs. John Sherwood
1884

Dinner Is
Served

good dinner is better than a fine coat.

—*"Dame Curtsey's"*
Book of Novel Entertainments
for Every Day in the Year
Ellye Howell Glover
1907

 olite, humorous, vivacious, speculative, dry, sarcastic, epigrammatic, intellectual, and practical people all meet around a dinner-table, and much agreeable small-talk should be the result.

—*Manners & Social Usage*
Mrs. John Sherwood
1882

The success of a dinner is readily judged by the manner in which conversation has been sustained.

—*American Etiquette and Rules of Politeness*
A. E. Davis
1882

It is only the very young girl at her first dinner-party whom it is difficult to entertain. At her second dinner-party, and thereafter, she knows the whole art of being amusing. All she has to do is listen; all we men have to do is tell her about ourselves.

—*If I May*
A. A. Milne
1921

You can not know what harm you may do your guests by placing wine before them. You may create in your friend an appetite for strong drink; you may renew a passion long controlled.

—*American Etiquette
and Rules of Politeness*
A. E. Davis
1882

Don't bite into a whole peach at the table the same as you would if you were out under the tree. When eating grapes don't blow the pits into the plate and all over the table.

—The Modern Hostess
Christine Terhune Herrick
1908

When a meal is concluded, it is most reprehensible to push away the last plate used and brush the crumbs on the cloth into little heaps.

—Encyclopedia of Etiquette
Emily Holt
1916

The Suitable Toast

Oh WHAT A DAY WE ARE HAVING!
come, here's a toast
A JOLLY XMAS TO YOU

The cup was filled to the brim with wine, ale, or mead, on the top of which would float a piece of toasted bread. After putting his lips thereto, the host would pass the cup to the guest of honour on his right, and he after drinking would pass it on to the neighbour on his right hand. In this manner the cup would circulate round the table. . . . Every one having taken a sip, the cup came back finally to the host, who drained it, and then swallowed the piece of toast in honour of all his guests.

Such was the origin of "toasts."

—*Inns, Ales and Drinking*
Customs of Old England
Frederick W. Hackwood
1909

By the bread and salt, by the water and wine,
Thou art welcome, friend, at this board of mine.

—*Waes Hael*
Edithe Lea Chase and
Capt. W. E. P. French
1903

I thank you for your welcome, which was cordial,
And your cordial, which was welcome.

—Anonymous

The ornament of a house is the guests who frequent it.

—Anonymous

Here's to the hostess who has worried all day,
　　And trembled lest everything go the wrong way;
May the grace of contentment possess her at once,
May her guests—and her servants—all do the right stunts.

—Francis Wilson, in
Prosit: A Book of Toasts
compiled by Clotho
1904

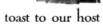

A toast to our host
　　And a song from the short and tall of us,
May he live to be
　　The guest of all of us!

—Anonymous

Dancing is wonderful training for girls. It's the first way you learn to guess what a man is going to do before he does it.

—*Kitty Foyle*
Christopher Morley
1939

The waltz is a dance of quite too loose a character, and unmarried ladies should refrain from it altogether, both in public and private; very young married ladies, however, may be allowed to waltz in private balls, if it is very seldom, and with persons of their acquaintance.

—*The Gentleman and Lady's
Book of Politeness*
Mme Celnart
1835

To sum up, the requisites of an agreeable ball are a well-bred hostess, good ventilation, good music, a good supper, guests who know their duties and not too large a number of them.

—*Sensible Etiquette of the Best Society*
Mrs. H. O. Ward
1878

ΠΦΩ

DANCES

7. North - McGill

8. Fisher - Yingst

9. X X

10. Kelsey - Madison

11. Stanton - Schneible

12. X X

6. X X

Learn to dance before you come out. Being a good dancer may not make you a belle, but treading on the stags' toes will certainly prevent you from becoming one.

—*No Nice Girl Swears*
Alice-Leone Moats
1933

Young ladies ought not to accept invitations for every dance. The fatigue is too wearing, and the heated faces that it induces too unbecoming.

—*Sensible Etiquette of the Best Society*
Mrs. H. O. Ward
1878

Waltz me around again, Willie, around and around and around,
The music is dreamy, it's peaches and creamy,
Oh! don't let my feet touch the ground!

—Will D. Cobb
1906

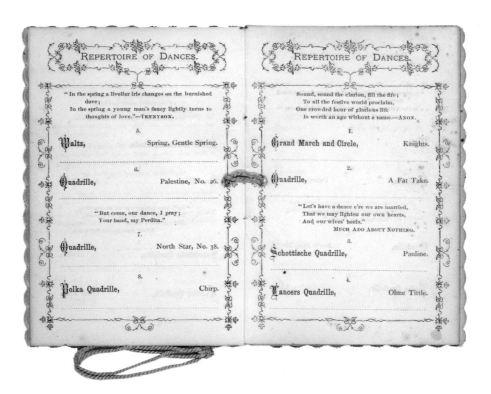

REPERTOIRE OF DANCES.

"In the spring a livelier iris changes on the burnished
dove;
In the spring a young man's fancy lightly turns to
thoughts of love."—TENNYSON.

5.

Waltz,   Spring, Gentle Spring.

6.

Quadrille,   Palestine, No. 26.

"But come, our dance, I pray;
Your hand, my Perdita."

7.

Quadrille,   North Star, No. 38.

8.

Polka Quadrille,   Chirp.

REPERTOIRE OF DANCES.

Sound, sound the clarion, fill the fife;
To all the festive world proclaim,
One crowded hour of glorious life
Is worth an age without a name.—ANON.

1.

Grand March and Circle,   Knights.

2.

Quadrille,   A Fat Take.

"Let's have a dance e're we are married,
That we may lighten our own hearts,
And our wives' heels."
MUCH ADO ABOUT NOTHING.

3.

Schottische Quadrille,   Pauline.

4.

Lancers Quadrille,   Ohne Tittle.

The dances should be arranged beforehand, and, for large halls, programmes are printed with a list of the dances. A ball usually opens with a waltz, followed by a quadrille, and these are succeeded by galops, lancers, polkas, quadrilles and waltzes, in turn.

—*American Etiquette
and Rules of Politeness*
A. E. Davis
1882

It is a girl's prerogative——whether a man's feet ache and he is breathless or not——to refuse to stop dancing until a dance has come to an end.

—*Good Manners for All Occasions*
Margaret E. Sangstep
1904

F lirtation comes under the head of morals more than of manner; still, it may be said that ball-room flirtation, being more open, is less dangerous than any other.

—*Sensible Etiquette of the Best Society*
Mrs. H. O. Ward
1878

R.S.V.P. (Répondez s'il vous plaît)
Answer, if you please

Costume de signeur
Full dress in character

Fête champêtre
A rural entertainment

Bal masqué
A masquerade ball

E.V. (En ville)
In the town or city

Soirée dansante
Dancing party

—Glossary of French phrases
found in invitations
*American Etiquette and Rules
of Politeness*
A. E. Davis
1882

t seems fitting that a book about traditions of the past should be decorated with period artwork. In that spirit, the art in *The Pleasure of Your Company* has been taken from personal collections of original nineteenth- and early-twentieth-century calling cards and other paper treasures of the time.

The endpapers and chapter openings contain patterns reproduced from some of our favorite vintage wallpapers.